A Woggle of Witches

A Woggle of Witches

BY ADRIENNE ADAMS

NEW YORK
CHARLES SCRIBNER'S SONS

This book published simultaneously in
the United States of America and in Canada
Copyright under the Berne Convention

1 3 5 7 9 11 13 15 17 19 RD/P 20 18 16 14 12 10 8 6 4 2
13 15 17 19 RD/C 20 18 16 14

Printed in the United States of America

Library of Congress Catalog Card Number 70-161536

ISBN 0-684-12506-4 (cloth)
ISBN 0-684-15331-9 (paper)

To Esther Reno

In a dark, dense forest the witches live,
sleeping safely in the branches of tall trees.
On a certain night, when the moon is high,
one calls, "Wake up. Time for the feast is come!"

The forest rings with the sound of their high voices.
"I'm ravenous. I hope it's bat stew!"
"It is! Give me more!"

"Leave the dishes. It's time to go!"
"Shh," one whispers. "Want to wake up the world?"

Out in the open and free of the trees,
the witches are ready for take-off.
''Run! Run! Straddle the broom!''
Up into the dark sky and away they go.

Zo-o-o-m!
"Tie on your hats!"

"Wheee------------"

"Let's make a ring around the moon!"

"Time for a rest now, and what a spot for it."
"The view—it's marvelous!"

"What's next?"

"Everybody off! Back to earth we go."

Down, down they sail, landing light as feathers
in a field of corn.

"What is that coming our way?"
"Oh, mercy, what—on—earth?"

"It's a parade of those monsters!"
And they hide, however they can.

"Let's get out of here!" they cry.
All quivering and quaking,
they leap on their brooms,
and slant toward the sky.

They sail back to the safety of the forest.

"I'm starved. Are there any leftovers?"
"Build up the fire. Catch more bats!"
"Bring out the spiderweb bread!"

Then, one by one, when the night is spent,
They climb to their treetop beds.
"Sleep tight, everybody."